One day Mum and Rob and I went to the country.

We had a picnic. Mum said if we were
lucky we might see some ducks or geese.

The Swan

Virginia Mayo

For my children, Robert and Elizabeth

A Red Fox Book

Published by Random House Children's Books
20 Vauxhall Bridge Road, London SW1V 2SA

A division of Random House UK Ltd
London Melbourne Sydney Auckland
Johannesburg and agencies throughout the world

Copyright © Virginia Mayo 1993

1 3 5 7 9 10 8 6 4 2

First published by Hutchinson Children's Books 1993

Red Fox edition 1996

Printed in China

RANDOM HOUSE UK Limited Reg. No. 954009

ISBN 0 09 923751 2

We were very lucky. We saw a *swan*.

He swam very close to me. 'Hello,' I said.

Mum told me that swans fall in love and stay together all their lives. If they are parted, the one left behind is so sad that it pines away and dies.

Then I noticed a fisherman and his little boy.
Their line broke and the fisherman threw it back
in the water.

Mum was angry. She said the swans could get tangled
in his line and the lead weights could poison them.

I thought perhaps the man didn't know that he might
hurt the swans; so I told him.

'Mind your own business!' he said.

Back at home I told Mum that I didn't understand how anyone could hurt animals.

I thought about my swan and how he had looked at me as if I was his friend.

That night I had a dream.

Someone tapped at my window.

When I woke up, for a moment I didn't know where
I was. Then I remembered my dream.

Mum came in to get me dressed. 'Look,' she said.
'A swan's feather. It must have caught on your clothes.'

Later that summer we went back to the river. We took
a picnic. Mum said if we were lucky we might see
some swans.

We were *very* lucky. We saw a mum and a dad and six babies!
  'Swans fall in love and stay together all their lives,'
I told Rob.
  They swam up close to show me their babies . . .

. . . and they looked right at me as if they knew I was their friend.